Kasey's Poodle Skirt

brought to life by Sandy De Young

illustrated by Kathy Lee

this book belongs to

_____

This book is dedicated to my
wonderful daughters,

Kelly and Kasey.

Their laughter, their zest for life,
and their fabulous sense of adventure
brighten my world.

It was Halloween, and Kasey's class was getting ready for their annual costume parade at school. This was Kasey's favorite day of school, and she was eager to wear her adorable new costume.

She put on her pink poodle skirt with a white fuzzy poodle and shiny jeweled leash sewn on the front. To complete her outfit, she wore black and white saddle shoes and a gray sweater with a big initial K on the front! She beamed with pride as she marched with her friends in the parade, smiling as she listened to the parents cheering them on from the sidelines.

Kasey won the best costume award, and from that day on, she begged her mom to wear her poodle skirt every day. She wore her skirt to the market, to school, out to dinner, and out to play in the neighborhood. Every night, she would place the poodle skirt at the end of her bed so that it would be ready to hop right back into in the morning. She absolutely adored her poodle skirt!

One night something woke Kasey with a start. She heard a quiet bark and felt a soft paw nudging her cheek. She opened her eyes to find a fluffy poodle snuggled up to her, looking right into her big blue eyes!

"Oh my! Who are you?" said a very surprised Kasey.

"My name is Pierre, and I am the poodle that lives on your skirt. Would you like to join me for some adventures tonight?" the poodle asked.

"Oh, that sounds fun, but I'm a little nervous," said Kasey.

"Don't worry, you will have the time of your life!" exclaimed Pierre.

With that, Kasey hopped out of bed, and off they went. They headed to the local train that would take them to their first adventure. The conductor welcomed them aboard the shiny silver train and they were off.

After a quick ride through the city, Kasey and Pierre arrived at the skating rink.

The lights sparkled on the white ice, and lively music played throughout the rink. Kasey changed into a pretty, pink skating dress with silver sparkles, laced up her skates, and headed straight to the ice. Pierre was a graceful skater and taught Kasey dances steps, spins, and jumps. Her eyes were twinkling as she glided across the ice, dancing to the beat of the music.

One, two, three; one, two, three; head up, back arched, and toes pointed! Kasey imagined herself skating in the Olympics with her fantastic partner, hearing the roar of applause from the audience as they twirled around the ice. She could have skated all night, but Pierre assured her there was more fun to be had.

Pierre and Kasey headed toward their next adventure. Pierre knew how much Kasey loved animals, so he took her to the zoo to meet his many animal friends. When they arrived at the front gate, it was very quiet. Pierre barked a few words, and all of a sudden monkeys, giraffes, and lions surrounded them. The animals were thrilled to see Pierre and excited to show Kasey around their home. In order to get the best view, Kasey hopped on the gigantic giraffe's back, and off they went. She had never been up so high and was thrilled when they grabbed delicious berries hanging from the tops of the trees!

Kasey's first stop was the monkey's home. She raced the monkeys up and down the trees, shared their bananas, and played catch with the banana peels. The monkeys told her how they tried to play catch with the visitors, but when they threw the peels out to the crowd, they all squealed with surprise and ducked for cover. This made the monkeys laugh and laugh!

The next stop was the lion's den where Kasey was greeted with an enormously loud roar. She jumped in the air with fright and then saw all the lions rocking back and forth on their backs, laughing and purring like playful kittens. Wide-eyed and speechless, she realized all her friends were playing a joke on her, and she joined in on the fun. Kasey loved her time at the zoo, but it was getting late. Kasey hugged her new friends goodbye. She couldn't wait to visit again and swing from the trees with the monkeys, and she would never let the roar of those big kittens scare her again! She thanked the giraffe for the ride, and Pierre and Kasey headed back to the train.

Kasey had such a fun night, and she loved her new friend, Pierre. They arrived home safe and sound, and Kasey snuggled back into bed. "Thanks for a magnificent night, Pierre!" said Kasey. She kissed him on the nose and fell asleep with a big smile on her face.

In the morning, Kasey's mom gently woke her up with a big hug. "Wake up, little monkey. It's time for school!"

"Oh, Mom, speaking of monkeys, I had the most wonderful time last night. You won't believe what happened!" As Kasey cheerfully described her exciting adventure with Pierre, her mom looked at her with love in her eyes, listening to every word.

"What an incredible night you had, Kasey! That is a dream you will always remember!"

Kasey wondered to herself, *Was this really a dream? Did I imagine all this? It seemed so real!* "Oh well," said Kasey. "If it was a dream, it was the best dream I have ever had!"

As she got out of bed, she reached for her poodle skirt and looked for Pierre. The skirt was just as she had left it last night with the poodle in place—nothing had changed!

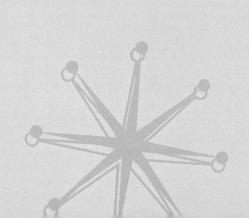

"Wow, I guess it was a dream. I will miss Pierre, but I will never forget my exciting night!"

As she was putting her poodle skirt on, she was feeling a bit sad. She already missed Pierre. She then heard a quiet bark and looked down on her skirt. Pierre looked up at Kasey and gave her a little wink. "Thanks for a fabulous night, Kasey. See you next time!"

The End

Proof

Made in the USA
Columbia, SC
12 February 2018